Library of Congress Cataloging-in-Publication Data Available

2 4 6 8 10 9 7 5 3 1

Published in 2005 by Sterling Publishing Co., Inc.
387 Park Avenue South, New York, NY 10016
Copyright © 2005 by Adam Relf

Distributed in Canada by Sterling Publishing
c/o Canadian Manda Group, 165 Dufferin Street
Toronto, Ontario, Canada M6K 3H6

Printed in Belgium
All rights reserved

Sterling ISBN 1-4027-2756-9

Fox
Makes Friends

Adam Relf

Sterling Publishing Co., Inc.
New York

Fox sat in his room.
He was bored.
"I know," he said.
"I need a friend."

Fox picked up his net and went to see his mom.
"I'm going to catch a friend," he declared.
"You can't catch friends," Mom explained.
"You have to *make* friends."
So Fox put down his net and
set off to make a friend.

"What can I make a friend out of?"
he thought.
He picked up some sticks, an apple, and
some nuts and fixed them all together.
At last he had a brand new friend
standing in front of him.

"Are you my friend?" Fox asked,
but the friend said nothing.
"Can you come and play?" he said,
but the friend didn't move. "Maybe he's
too small," Fox thought. "I need to make
a bigger friend!"

Just then a rabbit ran by. "Excuse me," said Fox. "I'm trying to make a friend but this one is too small. Can you help me make a bigger one?"

"Okay," said Rabbit.

They worked together and picked up a turnip,
some tomatoes, and some twigs. They stuck them
all together and had a bigger friend
standing before them.
"Will you be our friend?" they asked,
but there was no answer.

"Can you come and play?" they said,
but the friend just stood there.
"Maybe he's still too small,"
said Rabbit.

A moment later Fox and Rabbit
heard giggling in the treetops.
It was a squirrel.
"What a mess you two are
making!" he laughed.
"Well, if you can do
better, come down and
help us!" said Fox.
"Okay," said Squirrel.

This time all three of them set to work.
They picked a huge pumpkin, a turnip,
some branches, and some apples.
They put them all together and had
the biggest friend they could make.
"Are you our friend?" they asked.
"Please can you come and play?"
But there was no reply.

Finally they all gave up.
"Oh, well," said Fox. "I suppose I will never be able to make a friend."

Just then Fox's mother
came by.
"Hello," she said. "Who are
all your new friends?"
"Oh," said Fox. "My plan
didn't work. We made friends
but they won't play with us."
"Not them!" giggled his mother.
"These friends!" she said,
pointing to Squirrel
and Rabbit.

Fox looked over at Squirrel and
Rabbit and suddenly realized
that he had been making
friends all along!

So Fox, Squirrel, and Rabbit played for the rest of the day, and they stayed friends forever.